Numbers

Ruth Partis

Published in the United Kingdom
TAUP UK
Sheerness
Kent

enquiries@taup.uk

Table of Contents

AGM -The Minutes of the Meeting

The President of the WI adjusted her hat and stood to address the meeting.

'Welcome everyone. Firstly I must apologise for the secretary's and the treasurer's absence tonight.'

'I also regret that none of the committee and very few of the members are here, it was a waste to book the school hall really.'

'Before I continue, I would like the meeting minuted.' she looked around her, 'Oh dear, I'll have to write them myself wont I?'

'Anyway, I would like it minuted, that if any food is left over and taken home for future use, it must only be by members who have freezers.'

'I hate to speak ill of the dead, but I do think that Mrs Parkinson could have told us that the mince pies left over from the Christmas party were only stored in Tupperware until the Harvest Supper. I'm sure that the rest of the committee, when they come out of hospital, will agree with me.'

'I am not going to ask members to stand for two minutes silence in memory of all those who have died, as I'm hoping to get the meeting over in time to watch 'Crimewatch' as I understand we're going to get a special mention.'

'I'm afraid I don't have the minutes of the last meeting, as the book was destroyed, along with everything else, in the unfortunate fire that we had in the village hall during our last meeting. Various people in the village have taken the opinion that 'How to be a Fire Eater' was not a suitable talk and demonstration for the WI. I have had to point out that we are all here to be educated, and if we don't try different skills, how will we know that they are unsuitable.'

'I have received a charming letter from the Chief Fire Officer thanking us for the tea that we gave his men while they were fighting the blaze. He adds that it was not our fault at all that the wind changed and burnt out the whole High Street while they were drinking it.'

'I would like to thank Mrs Jolly and Mrs Jones for the speed in which they got the tea urn out of the hall; it was in fact the only thing saved from the whole place. I understand from Mrs Jolly's son that

1

she hopes to have the bandages off in a few weeks.'

'The secretary phoned me from her hospital bed this morning and tended her resignation, but I'm sure she will re-consider once the botulism starts to respond to treatment.'

'The treasurer, who like me doesn't eat mince pies, appears to be on holiday. I had hoped that she would be here tonight, but this morning I received a postcard from Spain from her. Sadly all the records of the WI's bank account were destroyed in the fire, but it looks like we are going to be busy fund-raising this Autumn, as the bank tells me that we have only 28p in our current account. They also insist that we do not have a deposit account. These banks can be so unhelpful, just because we have lost all the records in a fire.'

' If indeed we do only have 28p in the bank I am a little puzzled as there was at least £600 pounds in the account this time last year and we have been quite successful with our fund-raising. I recall that sales of cakes went very well at the Harvest Supper, certainly all the mince pies went at 20p each, and no-one asked for a refund.'

'I know that we did incur expenses on our outing to Brighton last month, when the driver was incapable of driving and we had to get the train home. I had understood that the money was to be re-funded by the coach company, but perhaps it hasn't arrived yet.'

'I still don't know what was wrong in giving the man his tip of a bottle of whiskey when we arrived in Brighton. I know he was distressed by our singing, and comb and paper band, but who would have expected him to have a drink problem.'

'Anyway our treasurer is bound to sort it all out when she gets home. I understand her husband, who owned the now burnt out shop next to the hall, has gone with her. I did hear that the shop was about to go bankrupt, but when I met the insurance assessor the other day he told me that there was a lot of expensive stock out in the stockroom that we hadn't seen. Sadly it was all lost in the fire.'

'I do hope they enjoy their holiday, they can't be planning to stay away long as I noticed a 'For Sale' sign going up on their house yesterday and of course, he is the collector for the village Christmas Club and will want to be here for the pay out next month.'

'Lastly, I invite you all...' she looks at her meagre audience. 'To our next meeting, It will be held in this hall and the speaker, a Mrs

Sharpe, will be 'Acupuncture – trying it out yourself'. The competition will be for a home-made pin cushion.'

'Now ladies, as there is no other business, don't forget to put your name down for the hospital visiting rota… and thank you all for coming. Now before we go let's have a cup of tea… and a mince pie.'

Boys in the Band

She gave up everything to follow them
To hear them every day
She only worked to earn the cash
To get in to hear them play.
And her friends and relations
Could never understand
Why she couldn't keep her mind off
The boys in the band.

She spent all her money
Buying them cigarettes and beer
She ironed all their trousers
And carried all their gear
And her friends and relations
Could never understand
Why she couldn't keep her eyes off
The boys in the band.

They let her handle their instruments
She'd help with button or zip
She'd do anything to please them
And she had a steady grip
And her friends and relations
Could never understand
Why she couldn't keep her hands off
The boys in the band.

And now you can still find her
In her golden age
Still standing mesmerised
At the side of the stage
And her sons and her grandsons
They all understand
Because each and everyone of them are
The boys in the band.

Chicken

The man had worked late and the night was very warm. He'd seen some awful things at work and his mind was a whirl. He had finally got to bed and to sleep long after his wife and young daughter.

It was still dark when he was woken by the cockerel crowing. He got out of bed angrily and went to the door and threw out a shoe towards the bird. He could see a tiny line of purple on the horizon but it was nowhere near morning yet. He went back to bed and lay still for a while, enjoying the feeling that he did not have to work today and could go back to sleep if only that damned bird would let him.

There was silence for about a quarter of an hour. He had just returned to his dreams when the cockerel crowed again. This time there were lines of light pink streaking across the sky. With a sigh he got out of bed again. It was light enough to see his wife this time, and she was still asleep. He wondered why the cockerel didn't wake her, because if the baby cried she would be awake at once ready to feed her. He looked at the baby too. She had just started to sleep through the night and was peacefully asleep in her crib beside their bed. He picked up his one shoe and crept outside to retrieve the one he had thrown at the cockerel. He put the shoes on to protect his feet from the harsh ground.

When the cockerel crowed for the third time it did so very loudly. The dawn really had arrived and the bird, which had only just got old enough to crow, tipped his head back and crowed as loud as he could. He never brought his head back down again. The man had him by the throat. In a second his neck was broken and a sharp knife took off his head. The man hung the bird outside the door, its blood dripping on the stone path. He knew his wife would be sad. This bird had been a really beautiful one, and she had turned it into a bit of a pet, that was why they hadn't already eaten it when it proved to be a male. She would cook it though, with a bit of red wine and a few vegetables from the market. They would eat well tonight. Maybe they should invite someone over to share it with them. He went back into the house, kicking his shoes off. There was blood on his hands but he couldn't be bothered to wash. He rubbed his hands together

Numbers

and spread the blood up his wrists till it felt dry.

He climbed back into bed. His wife stirred slightly but she was still sound asleep. He snuggled down towards her. He would not get up until the morning got too hot. The silence was enveloping him and he relaxed, dropping straight off to sleep, safe in the knowledge that he would not have to rise again.

Daffodils

On the last day I came to see you
It was wet.

The path was muddy
And I picked just the flowers
I could reach without getting my shoes dirty.

Nine daffodils.

I didn't know it was the last time I would see you
Or I would have searched the garden
And picked every wet flower and pretty leaf
And each fruit bud and ornamental grass,
And hired a juggernaut to bring them to you.

But I didn't know.

Ellen's Friend

Ellen hated the home. She hated the staff, she hated her room, she hated the food, but most of all she hated herself. Her stupid body had let her down and she had been forced to leave the home she had lived in for fifty years and move into this soulless, colourless, home. It was clean to the point of sterility and smelt of hand cleaner, surface cleaner and bloody everything cleaner. It was too warm at night when she was trying to get to sleep and too cold during the day when they opened the windows to let the air in.

She hated the shared television that was always too quiet to hear properly and didn't show her favourite programmes.

She was now beginning to lose her mind too. After breakfast, she had spent all morning trying to remember the name of her youngest grandson. There was a lovely picture of him in a university cap and gown on her dressing table, but she just couldn't remember his name. It would be no good asking these pretend nurses. They would just smile and say 'Don't worry dear.'

It was all right for them. They hadn't broken their hip replacement or forgotten what their youngest grandson was called.

It was sometimes painful for her to move at all and wherever she went they wanted her to be somewhere else, 'Come and have dinner', 'Why don't you sit next to Joan and have a chat?' or 'Would you like to knit some blanket squares?'

What she really wanted to do was to sit in her room and sulk, but they always wanted her to be busy.

One of the other old ladies had died and her relatives had delivered a new wooden bench for the garden and it was placed outside Ellen's window. She decided that it was meant for her and took to sitting out on warm afternoons, in the shade of the huge holly bush. She found that if she was outside the pretend nurses would leave her alone. Sitting, doing nothing outside, was accepted as an activity.

Ellen was amazed one afternoon when someone came and sat beside her. She thought it must be a new resident, because she didn't recognise her, but the other woman smiled and said' It's me Ellen, don't you remember me?'

It was Mary, Ellen's childhood friend. They had done everything together when they were girls. She had helped her through school and at home when her grandmother had been in a bad mood or when her mother had one of her headaches. Ellen was so pleased to see her. She couldn't remember when they had parted as youngsters, but Mary said it didn't matter.

She could remember when they had first met. Ellen had been in trouble for stealing sugar lumps from the pantry and was hiding at the end of the garden by the compost heap. Mary had appeared and they had talked, made daisy chains and picked a bunch of dandelions. Ellen's grandma had laughed at the flowers and told Ellen that she would wet the bed, but she hadn't. Mary and her had laughed about it the next day.

Every afternoon was then spent in happy conversation. Mary had always been a great listener and she still was. Ellen told her everything about her life and she found that she could remember it completely. She might not remember what she had eaten for lunch, but she could recall her time at school, especially when Mary and her had pretended to be ill and got sent home, missing a spelling test.

She told Mary all about starting work at fifteen in a sweet shop, where she had met Leslie and every moment of their wedding day.

She'd been an only child herself and their four children had arrived close together and she had loved the bustling chaotic home that they'd shared. She told Mary about all the pets. The three legged dog, the cat that had kittens in the airing cupboard, the rabbit that escaped when they had only had it two days and the goldfish that kept jumping out of its tank. She wished that Mary had been in her life then, but she had just been too busy for friends.

The days turned into weeks and they sat side by side on the bench. The weather was mild and they were able to go out most days.

When they run out of things to say, they just sat in comfortable silence. They had to go inside for meals, but afterwards it was always straight outside. Ellen's hip was not hurting so much and the staff were happy to leave them in peace.

Numbers

At night Mary would creep into Ellen's room and stay until she went to sleep and in the morning would be waiting ready for breakfast.

One night Ellen was restless and Mary stayed by her bedside, not speaking, but smiling silently as she finally went to sleep. Ellen did not wake up, she just stopped living in the night and died.

And Mary, well Mary just wasn't there in the morning either.

Five Hundred Words

"Five hundred words!" he almost shouted.

"All I asked for from you all was a 500 word essay on one aspect of your chosen Dickens novels – what had you learned about life in Dicken's time?"

The boy remained silent, Mr Billings continued "And what did you give me – twenty-eight words – one sentence."

The boy still remained silent, his eyes fixed on the open note book in front of him.

"And what a sentence."

Mr Billings picked up the homework book and read aloud.

"From the book I learned that in Dickens' time there was not much to do in the evenings, but get drunk, dance on tables and count your money."

The boy went to speak, but Mr Billings leaning over him, waved his hand in front of his face, and the boy thought better of it.

The teacher continued "Now come on Jonathan, English student, tell the class which one of Charles Dickens' great novels did you choose to read?"

"It's Oliver."

"Charles Dickens did not write a book called Oliver."

"He did sir, my gran has the DVD."

Mr Billing inhaled deeply.

"Do you know what a book is Jonathan?"

"Yes Sir"

"Then go now, to the school library and find one –and make sure it has pages and print and is written by Charles Dickens please."

The boy rapidly left the room. Most of the class had been sitting in bemused silence, although one or two looked sheepishly as if they too had hoped to skip any actual reading.

The buzzer sounded for lunch and the teacher wearily told the class to leave, leaving their homework books in a pile in front of him.

Once the classroom was empty, he couldn't stop his mind going back to one of his own school days. He too was reading Oliver Twist and still blushed at the memory of asking in class why Bill Syke's dog Bullseye was named after a Quiz Show about darts. That had got him a detention and months of teasing from the rest of the class. He had hated the book ever since.

Maybe Jonathan should get away with his mistake.

Smiling, he looked through the homework, and began to compile a list of their chosen books, there were four *Oliver Twists*, six *Tale of two Cities*, three *Nicolas Nicklebys*, six *Old Curiosity Shops*, seven *Great Expectations*, two *A Christmas Carols* and lastly one *One Pair of Hands*.

Surprised, he looked at the cover of the book. It belonged to the girl who was the brightest in the class. He googled 'One pair of Hands' and discovered it was written by Monica Dickens.

He snapped the books shut and stood up. In the staffroom he made a coffee and decided it would be a good time to retire to his car in the car park and enjoy a quiet smoke. He knew he wasn't ever going to give up smoking – well not until he gave up teaching English.

Gamble (an outside chance)

I've never known if I should blame or thank the horse.

It was my mother's birthday. Not a day of celebration in our house, where days were all much the same. Go to school, come home for a tea of bread and butter, wait for mum to come home from work tired, dad to come home from work angry, hear him have a row with mum and go to the pub. Once the door had slammed I would go to bed and drift off to sleep to the sound of mum's crying.

However, this time her birthday fell on a Saturday and we always went shopping on Saturdays. Dad handed over the meagre housekeeping money late on a Friday night and mum and I rushed to the shops to spend every penny on food that would last the week. Keeping cash for fresh food later in the week was not an option, as the money would vanish from her purse for his midweek drinking sessions. Dad was not violent to mum, but when he was drunk he often stumbled against her. He was a huge bear of a man and easily weighed three times more than her. He had a foul tongue when he was drunk and no-one messed with him. Luckily he generally just ignored me, something that I was very thankful for.

As we were getting ready to go out on this day he appeared from the bedroom and called Mum over. He planted a noisy kiss on her cheek and handed her a grubby £5 note with instructions to treat herself for her birthday. She looked amazed and I guessed that this was a first. She took it rather reluctantly and asked if he wanted her to do him a favour. She obviously knew him well. What he wanted was for us to call in at the betting shop and put some money on a horse for him. He had it written down on an envelope so that mum would get it right. He handed it over and went back into the bedroom and shut the door.

Mum looked at the envelope. She had to put money on a horse called Rusty Rainbow that was running at 2.30 that day. Then she looked in the envelope and counted the money. There was £50. Mum didn't say a word but I could tell what she was thinking. £50, twice as much as we had to do the weeks shopping and ten times as much as he had given her for her birthday.

She never said a word on the way into town.

It was a long walk, but she never said a word, I imagined that I could hear her brain whirring, mine certainly was.

Outside the betting shop she stopped and I could tell she was making her mind up what to do. I was too young to go in but I saw her through the open door. She was talking to the girl behind the counter for a long time. When she came out, I asked her what she had done.

'I have decided to try gambling' she explained. 'His stupid horse is favourite and even if it wins it wont pay out much, so I've put all the money on an outsider. There is one running called Lily's Birthday.'

My mum's name is Susan.

We went and did the shopping and we spent her birthday money. She bought a mauve cardigan for herself in a charity shop, and some value bubble bath and a chocolate sponge cake in Tesco. We did not speak about the horses. We sat in the precinct on one of the concrete seats and ate the cake. We ate all of it and we even spared a few crumbs for the pigeons that we soon attracted. I'd never eaten half a cake before and I don't think Mum had either. After that we sat and waited. We both knew what we were waiting for, but we still didn't speak about it. I didn't see that we could ever go home if Dad's horse won.

We sat there until three o'clock then made as if to go home. She left me outside the betting shop with the bags of shopping. She was gone for ages and I began to feel really sick and wished that I hadn't eaten the cake.

She came out with a dazed look on her face and hurried me away.

'Are we going home?' I asked.

'Yes' she said 'His horse didn't win.'

The relief swept over me like a huge cold wave. We were safe; she had got away with her moment of madness. Dad would be cross, but not with Mum, not with me.

She picked up the shopping bags and went off ahead of me. Over her shoulder I heard her say 'My one did.'

I tried to ask questions but she shushed me 'Don't say a word.'

I never did find out how much she won, but I did see her take a book from beside her bed. It was one of the romantic novels that my dad despised.

She inserted her fortune in notes one at a time between the pages. Then put the book back and placed another heavier one on top.

It stayed there untouched for ages. Life went on exactly the same until the first day of the school summer holidays.

Dad went off to work and the minute he was out of sight she gave me a carrier bag and told me to put everything I cared about in it. I didn't have much in the way of toys that weren't broken but I soon filled the bag. She had already packed my clothes, she must have been preparing them for weeks they were all clean, ironed and folded very small. Within twenty minutes we were out the house. Instead of walking into town we took the bus and went into her favourite charity shop where apparently they had kept a suitcase for her. Paying them from one of the notes she packed our clothes into the case and she bought me a new coat and gave them my old one. Her happiness was contagious and we virtually skipped to the station.

At the station she bought us tickets to a place I'd never heard of, that became our new home.

I never saw my dad again. I don't think he even looked for us, because we didn't change our names, just settled in. I went to a new school, Mum got a new job and for a few years everything was all right.

There was food on the table all week and mum was able to get herself a few little treats. Unfortunately some of her little treats were bottles of sherry.

My dad had been a drunk because he took too much beer, it was a long time before I realised that Mum was a drunk too. In time she began to smell of sherry all the time and the food on the table started to come second to the bottles lined up ready for the bin men. Then she started to take them out with her to put in litter bins so that I didn't see how many there were.

Then she lost her job because she fell over at work a few times. I was old enough to leave school and started to look for ways to get away myself.

There was no big win on the horses for me, but I managed to get a lowly job in a hotel that was poorly paid, but did give me accommodation. It still didn't take me long to pack and she let me take the charity shop suitcase. As I went she gave me £20 and a kiss laced with sherry. Tears were streaming down her face and she kept saying how very sorry she was. She never asked why or where I was going.

My escape was as good as hers. She went north, leaving my dad in the south and I went east leaving her in the north. I've done OK, bit by bit, I was used to living frugally, so was able to save and move on successfully.

I've never got a taste for alcohol and I've never put so much as 10p on a horse, outsider or not, and I still don't know if I want to thank or blame the horse.

He used to buy me roses

He used to buy me roses
And freesias which was nice
Today he brought me a cauliflower
That was reduced to half it's price.

We used to dine at Gordon's
Champagne and truffles we'd eat
Today he bought me a bag of chips
And we ate them in the street.

He once took me to Paris
To Venice and to Rome
Today he took me to Tesco
And then he brought me home.

He used to get me diamonds
And French designer frocks
Today he gave me a plastic spoon
That was free in a cereal box.

He used to buy me roses
And presents by the score
And now he gives me everything
And I couldn't ask for more.

Isis, the Witch's Cat

Two men had come to the cottage one morning and taken the witch away. The cat had hidden firstly under the bed, and then she'd slipped out quite unnoticed. Her shiny black body pressed flat against the grass as she moved silently across the garden. The men had taken the witch away without a backwards glance at her.

For those first few days it was hard for the cat to find food. She caught plenty of moths and a few mice, but she was always hungry and slept only fitfully, without the pleasant feeling a full tummy gave her. Then one day, following the scent of meat, she'd found a house with a dish of cat food outside the back door. She'd barely been able to eat it for purring and she felt so good afterwards that she climbed high up in a tree to wash and watch the house for more food. Sure enough the lazy fat tabby cat that lived there never finished her meals and the thoughtful owner put the remains outside for her to eat later. The house was on the edge of an orchard that had long grass between the trees and the witch's cat decided to make the garden and orchard her new home.

The cat soon began to regain her full powers. Her glossy black fur grew thicker for the cold nights and her killing skills improved. Without the overwhelming hunger she could wait for bigger prey. Rabbits, pigeons and pheasants were soon as easy for her to catch as butterflies, as her eyes grew keener and her claws sharper. She increased her territory to include the whole of a nearby farm and it was here one spring morning that she took a weak newborn lamb. It tasted really good and as the sheep had another stronger lamb as well, the humans didn't notice the loss.

The cat kept well away from humans. They had taken away her mistress and they would have her too if she let them. At first she went back to the witch's house often. On one early visit she'd slipped in through the cat flap to find all the witches belongings stacked in the middle of the kitchen in boxes. Her clothes, books, herbs and potions were there. The cat had rubbed her whiskers against the witch's things, taking in her smell and remembering her touch, but the cat knew for sure that she wasn't coming back.

Days later she'd seen a big motor take everything away and the cottage had been left totally empty. The cat had stood in every room and yowled in sadness, before slipping out again to her new life.

One sunny morning she'd returned to find new washing on the line and inviting cooking smells coming from a window. She'd been surprised to find that she couldn't get through the cat flap. These new humans had made it smaller to keep her out. Her head just wouldn't go through, but her nose and whiskers twitched at the smell of humans. A little dejected she had slunk miserably away. The cottage would never be her home again.

She had always been a virtually invisible cat. It was not that people couldn't see her, more that they just didn't notice her. The witch had kept herself to herself and she'd learned as a kitten how not to be seen. But in her new life it was becoming difficult. She hunted at dawn and twilight, unless some prey threw themselves at her during the day, and suddenly people were beginning to be able to see her.

One afternoon she was sitting by the road, well hidden from sight, when a passing car hit a partridge, sending it spinning to her paws. It took just one bite to finish it off and she dragged it off to thicker cover to eat. As she went, she heard a shout and looking back she saw humans looking and pointing. She dropped the partridge and ran, her long powerful legs putting distance between her and the people until she felt safe again. She crept back later to retrieve the food, making sure that the humans had gone.

From that day she found it harder to keep hidden. People seemed to be looking for her. If ever she broke cover in daylight some human would be there, looking and pointing. Once when she crossed a road in the early hours of the morning, a woman cyclist actually screamed when she saw her. She couldn't understand it. True she had grown and become more muscular since she was a house cat, but she was still the same creature surely. Her head and jaws had become stronger and she knew that when she scratched the trees her marks were now much higher up the trunks, but she remembered sitting purring in front of the fire, and she would gladly go back to that life if she could. Large animals now gave her great respect, small ones fear. She was increasingly aware that she was big and black and magnificent. She no longer needed to hide in the farm and orchard. Nothing challenged her, dogs cowered as she growled at them and other cats eyed her with awe. She killed and ate anything she liked, chickens, ducks and hares. She learned to avoid geese, as they made such a noise. She started to travel further, sleeping in a different hideaway every day. Once she took an injured young deer on a motorway and ate it unseen in a ditch as cars sped past nearby. She was of course still under the witch's spell. She would not be caught, she would not die.

The cat still lives her lonely, but comfortable life. She's seen occasionally, but rarely filmed. One day she may find another witch who will turn her back into a house cat, but until then she's out there, slinking past our homes in the night, big and black and magnificent.

Juggling the Sponsorship.

The regulars down the pub used to give an audible groan every time Marty walked in with a piece of paper. The only way to avoid his long drawn out appeal to sponsor him for some hair brained scheme was to throw him a couple of pound coins quickly and add their names to his list.

He'd done them all 'Jeans for Genes', 'Denim for Diabetes', 'Children in Need', 'Help for Heroes.' You name it he'd done it. He had gone through October without alcohol and grown a moustache in November. He had a wardrobe of costumes that he donned when rattling his tin or bucket outside the supermarket. There was a monk's habit, a Tigger suit, a complete clown costume (including size 20 shoes) and even an imitation fur stone-man tabard with a huge plastic dinosaur bone.

He'd eaten pancakes against the clock (the clock won), been covered in green slime (that had taken weeks to wash out) and had abseiled down the side of the post office. He had unfortunately been sick on the way down, all over the regional organiser and the local mayor.

Everyone agreed that his heart was in the right place although they weren't always so sure about his brain. He lived with his gran and every Christmas raised money for her over 70's club to have a party. He used to put on the entertainment himself and his magic tricks were legendary. Unfortunately.

His trick of pulling a guinea pig out of a hat caused hilarity every time, especially the year the creature had gnawed through the bottom of the hat, and had been running around the hall for most of his act without him noticing. He always borrowed the animal from the small child that lived next door but she didn't like rabbits.

Once the Christmas events were over there was usually a bit of a lull in his fund-raising, but not last year. With the decorations still up he told the assembled New Year's Eve revellers that he had been able to get a place in The London Marathon. He was going to run for MacMillan Nurses and he was about to start training. He had proper printed sponsor forms this time and wanted pledges for miles rather than the 'Here's a couple of quid – now bugger off' type that he usually got.

Before anyone signed his form they wanted to know if he was doing it in costume, as that would undoubtedly slow him down.

It is worth noting here that Marty was not a man really built for speed. His gran's steak-and-kidney pies and the pub's hot pork sandwiches, with chips, had been adding to his waistline ever since his teens. He was also addicted to Mars bars and always bought one to eat on the way home from the pub. He felt he needed sustaining for the four minute walk back to his gran's house.

The regulars felt that they were pretty safe so the sponsor form was pinned up at the bar and soon quite generous amounts were being pledged. Marty had decided not to do it in too silly a costume, he wasn't quite as daft as he appeared. He would wear the charity's tee shirt, jogging trousers and proper running shoes. He was taking this event seriously.

A few nights later though, he was in the pub, trying to juggle a bag of peanuts and a bag of crisps, when he had a brilliant idea. He would juggle three balls for the whole 26 miles. That would slow him down, but he knew he wasn't going to break any records with his running, but he did like to please a crowd.

It took the pub regulars a few weeks to notice that Marty wasn't in the pub so often. They all kept thinking that he must have been in and they'd missed him, but the landlord put them straight. He'd met his gran in the butchers and she'd told him that Marty was busy training every night. The landlord put the sponsor form out of his customers reach so they couldn't reduce their promised amounts. Marty was a bit of a joke but he had to be admired, even if the pub's takings were down and the regular order of Mars bars were building up in the corner. All through January and February Marty's visits to the pub were short and sparse. He did buy some bottles to take home, and a few Mars bars, but he really only went in to count up his sponsors.

He didn't look very different, but anyone doing this much training must be doing something right, or so the regulars thought, as they worried about their money.

The day of the marathon finally came and the pub was packed early in the morning to watch the BBC coverage, although they didn't really expect to see Marty amongst the thousands taking part.

They didn't see him. He started off in the crowd walking along with everyone else. His training had really paid off. He was juggling, not three, but four balls. He had practised every night since New Year and he was perfect at it. He juggled as he walked the first mile but then other 'fun' runners around him started to run. Marty had not trained for this. Safe in his bedroom with bottled beer to keep him going and the TV to watch he had perfected just the juggling. After another mile as he gasped for breath he realised that he may have been wrong.

The pub regulars paid up their pledges. Some even put more in. Marty was a bit of a local hero really and he had made the TV news, as the St John's ambulance man had tried to revive him. They hadn't shown the paramedics shocking him, or the doctor shaking his head. Their news had only focused on the winners and the finishers.

They had a whip round at the pub after his funeral. They gave the money to his gran. She popped into the pub to collect it. As she enjoyed an 'on the house' sweet sherry she dipped into her shopping basket and handed over a sponsor form for an over 70's knit-a-thon.

Keeping the Secrets of Broadway

The road was re-opened at last. Residents and passing motorists had put up with the closure of the Broadway for more than six weeks and were pleased when they found it was open again. At least, they were to start with.

Rumours started almost at once about what had really gone on. The frequent and noisy deliveries by huge lorries after dark, while the work was carried out, had not really been what was expected to just resurface a road.

At last the intrepid news hounds at the local paper managed to get to the bottom of what was really happening. Local MP Joris Bohnson had volunteered the village to be used as a trial area for a new fast rail track. He lived on the Leas in Minster and the track ran underground from outside his home to Minster Broadway and came out near the fish and chip shop. This track, fractionally over a mile long, meant that one passenger, firmly strapped into a special seat, could cover the distance in 3.666 seconds. Heavier passengers took slightly longer, maybe 3.777 seconds.

The newspaper headline suggested that local MP Joris Bohnson had only let the system be installed so he could get his fish and chips home before they got cold. This accusation he vehemently denied, but he was not believed.

By the next day the national papers got hold of the story. Then, after the village was mentioned on 'Have I Got News for You?' and 'The News Quiz' visitors started arriving, demanding to see what the government had wasted their money on this time. Of course no-one knew what 'Super-rail' had really cost, but the guesses doubled at every telling. By the end of a week it was rumoured to be fifty billion pounds.

Questions were asked in parliament. On the BBC One O'clock News, Joris assured the public that he would not be resigning, so, everyone knew that his days were numbered. He had only got into parliament by standing for the 'None of the Above Party' at the previous election and, therefore, had no political friends to stand by him. It was just ten minutes after he assured his constituents that he would not be going that he went. Unusually, he was bodily thrown out of the building by the speaker, a spectacle not seen since Tudor times.

(Incidentally, now un-employed, he tried to get a job in the Minster Broadway newsagents, pointing out that he could be there in 3.777 seconds. They turned him down)

For a few days the Isle of Sheppey glowed in the media spotlight with visitors arriving to see, or indeed travel on, the wonderful 'Super-rail' even though the operator 'Verging' charged non-residents £249.99 return for the ride. Home-owners in The Broadway used their initiative and started charging people inflated prices to park in their drives, and to use their bathrooms. A small teashop in a tent was a great success for the first few days, until supplies ran out. Bottled drinking water became a luxury commodity that stranded drivers had to get, and gold jewellery and expensive watches often changed hands for the refilling of second-hand water bottles.

Then the first coaches started appearing and from that moment everything went wrong. Hordes of visitors totally blocked all the roads, not to mention both bridges! No-one could leave or get onto the island. The air ambulance had to be used for anyone who needed a hospital. Food supplies were dropped to the supermarkets by the Army's Chinook helicopters. People living in the far corners of the island became completely isolated, and even farm animals were going unfed.

Bicycles were using pavements, despite this having been banned under Section 72 of the 1835 Highways Act which prohibited this in, believe it or not, 1835. (Section 72 of the Highway Act 1835.) Bicycles, being the only means of transport were changing hands at vastly inflated prices. Any cycle left unattended was stolen and never seen again. Stranded car drivers either abandoned their cars or lived in them. The drains in the roads became rather primitive toilets and the smell became appalling.

The Prime Minister, Griff Rhys-Jones and Prince William visited and later that day a State of Emergency was declared, especially after Simon Cowell had promised a visit. Peter Andre cancelled after Katie Price turned up.

Just a few days after the first uncovering of the 'Super-rail' the army was called in. Oddly enough the short journey underground from the Leas to the shops in Minster Broadway was the only motorised movement available although the shops had no food and the chip shop had been the first to close. Mass evacuation of residents was started and gradually cars were moved from the roads. It took months to get the island almost back to normal. Many people had been airlifted out, and, having been housed in caravan parks on the north Kent coast, quite a few decided to stay there.

Morrisons and Iceland survived the crisis but Tesco never opened again. The building was turned into a centre for the poor and needy of the island. Joris Bohnson was installed there as a volunteer, but it was not a success. He proved to be so totally useless at this that he became a borough councillor.

As for the 'Super Rail', it was too expensive to remove so liquid concrete was poured into the entrances and it remains as a monument to stupidity.

Just what will Time Team make of that in three hundred year's time?

Listening Place.

I've been dreading this moment. This could be the very last time that I'm here on my special listening place. The house is sold now, totally empty, just faded curtains hanging at the windows and a small pile of papers by the front door. All the familiar sounds are changed now the furniture has gone. The heating boiler is silent, its steady hum no longer filling the house like a sleeping breathing dragon.

The stair carpet, old and worn and still dusty even after much hoovering, at least makes the listening place comforting. I sit down with my head against the smooth dark banister. I feel like a child again. I can't remember the first time I found it, I must have been very small. This bend in the stairs keeps you hidden, but still close to the hall beneath. From here, everything said in the kitchen could be heard, and in those days most things did seem to be said in the kitchen. The rest of the house was cold, with lino on the floors and loose slippery mats the only comfort for small bare feet. The dining room, with its grand, but draughty, French windows was used only for visitors and Christmas. The front room filled with huge ugly chairs was heated by an ancient gas fire that hissed so loud it virtually drowned out the radio that took pride of place in the corner. In the evenings my parents tended to sit at the kitchen table and talk, oblivious to the fact that I sat close by, listening. One blissful day a telephone was installed and placed in the hall, right under the listening place.

I learned everything from my evening's listening. I had to be careful not to ever disclose what I knew. I became good at acting surprised when things happened. I always knew little things like what was for dinner the next day, or who was coming to visit, but I heard important things too. I knew I was going to have a baby brother or sister months before my big sister Janet was told. I heard about my grandfather's illness and was quite prepared for his death. I had shed my tears alone in the listening place and was unable to cry when the news was given to me at breakfast one morning.

The telephone gave me an entirely new outlook, for I could hear my mother talk to my grandmother and to my aunts. I don't remember ever hearing my father talk on the phone, but on nights when he went out I found out many amazing things. I was quite shocked the first time I heard Mum criticise him, but I soon got used to it. She didn't love him at all and she only married him because of Janet. I heard about his meanness and coldness towards her. After one night when she cried for over an hour to her sister I sat shivering and crying too and I never felt quite the same about him.

As I got older I got more careful, once, just once, I had been caught lying on the listening place, after a tiring day there had been silence in the kitchen and I had fallen asleep. Mother had just picked me up and put me to bed without a word, but I had been terrified that it would happen again. Janet knew I was out of our bedroom most evenings, but she didn't care, she was just glad to get to sleep without my cold feet kicking at hers under the covers. I had to be alert once little Susie was born, she would cry out and my father would grumble, so Mum would rush up the stairs to her and I had to be quick to get out the way.

One January night our world ended. I had listened to Mum and Father in the kitchen, but she could not get him to talk. He wanted to read the paper and told her to go to bed and stop getting on his nerves. I was in bed and feigning sleep when he looked in a few minutes later. In the morning I was awoken by a terrible sound, it was Mum, she had picked Susie up out of her cot and she was cold and dead. Father pushed Janet and I into our school clothes and out the door, forcing us to leave our mother, who was on her knees wailing in the hall. We were too early for school and stood crying outside the locked gate until the headmaster arrived to let us in. When we got home, all signs of the baby were gone. It was as if she had never been. Mum was asleep in bed and our grandmother was baking in the kitchen. All the warm smells and tastes of a baking session were wasted on us, we ate the still warm cakes, but they tasted like sawdust and could hardly be swallowed.

Just days later I heard Mum tell her sister that our father was going to leave us. I was glad, but for all his coldness my Mum was distraught that he was going.

As a child I didn't understand what this meant, didn't know that we would have to leave the house and that divorce was a disgrace. I soon did know though, heard my Mum beg my grandmother for help, and be refused. I heard my parents talk stiffly about the house being sold and where Janet and I would live. My Father said that we should go with him as she obviously couldn't look after children, and that it was her fault Susie had died. I held my breath as Mum sobbed, only relaxing as I heard her regain her voice and say that 'No, he would not have us, ever'. Her voice was as cold and calm as his and I never heard that suggestion again.

The house was sold and on my last night I slept on my beloved listening place. There was nothing to hear, no-one was in the kitchen with Mum. She helped me to bed as the big clock, already in its packing case, struck midnight. The following day we moved to a small one bedroom cottage across the road from the house.

I never went back inside the house until today. Other people with other lives have lived here. I wonder if other little girls have discovered the listening place. I expected there to be echoes, that the joys and sorrows of this house would be audible, but there is just a loud silence that hurts the ears. I don't know why I am here now.

Softly, gradually I hear two people talking, they have come in through the kitchen. They are workmen, tool boxes in hand. They can't see me, I stay in the listening place as they go up and down the stairs, but they can't see me. They are talking quietly, they look as if they feel a little uneasy. The house is very cold, I hadn't noticed before, but they are shivering as they work. They are saying that the house is going to be knocked down. It will be turned into a row of modern town houses to match the ones built over the road where the cottages used to be. One of the workmen is older, looking out a window he tells his companion where the cottages used to be, before the fire that destroyed them. How sad it was that a young woman and her two daughters were burned alive just after they moved in. They had been trying to keep warm by leaving a gas ring on and a towel had fallen across the flame.

I'm not listening any more, my grief is overwhelming, the house is coming down, my listening place will be gone forever. Invisible tears stream down my face as I hear the men leave. I lie down on the carpet and curl up like a baby. It is comforting, and I want to spend just one more night here, in my listening place.

Merman

Dora opened the curtains. This was probably her favourite time of the day, and the reason that she still lived in the house. It was way too big for her now that Brian had died, but the view from her bedroom window was too special to lose. First, her own tidy front garden, a quite road, a stretch of beautifully cut grass and finally the beautifully golden beach and the sea.

She went down stairs to enjoy almost the same view from the living room. It was then that she noticed something on the beach. There were often dog walkers or even horse riders going along the water's edge, but this was something else.

She went into Brian's study without hesitation, although she hadn't been in there since her daughters had cleared all Brian's paperwork out for her. His telescope was still focused on the horizon where every morning he had logged the passing ships while he had his morning coffee.

She moved the telescope slightly and focused on the water's edge. She had dreaded that it was a washed up body, but she could see now that it was moving, although obviously in need of help. She wondered if it was a dolphin or even a large seal. Taking her mobile phone she hurried out the front door and across the grass.

She was amazed to find that there right, in front of her was a creature she didn't think existed. It had its back to her and was struggling to get back to the sea, but it was undoubtedly a mermaid. Long tangled hair fell down almost to its waist where instead of a bottom and legs was a huge scaly tail glistening in the sunshine.

Feeling stupid she called out, 'Hello – do you need any help?'

The startled creature's head turned round and they stared at each other in amazement. Matching the length of the hair down the back, a long curly grey beard covered the chest of what Dora now realized must be a merman.

He made another attempt to get back in the water, but Dora could see that he was injured, his right arm was hanging almost uselessly at his side.

'Your arm might be broken.' she said quietly and opened her phone to call for help. The terror in his eyes stopped her and she snapped it shut again.

'Please let me help you.' she asked.

He ignored her voice and lay down in the sand. He was plainly exhausted. Maybe ringing for an ambulance was not such a good idea. He would be terrified by it and she couldn't imagine the reaction he would get in Casualty. The merman shivered and she took off her cardigan and put it round his shoulders.

Whatever was she going to do?

Telling him not to worry she raced back across to her house. From the cupboard under the stairs she dragged out the wheelchair that Brian had needed in his last few months. She also took the throw off the settee. She also tried to ring her daughter that lived nearby but there was no reply. She decided not to leave a message. Whatever was she going to say?

He didn't struggle as she pulled him unto the wheelchair. He wasn't as heavy as she had expected, but longer, his tail kept falling off the footrest and pushing it across the sand was very difficult. Once the throw was wrapped round him he stopped shivering and he relaxed. It was a job to get him up the step and into the house but she finally managed it and took him into the lounge and rolled him onto the settee.

He looked wistfully out to sea and she tucked him up again with the throw round his tail.

She carefully took his arm and looked at it. It didn't appear to be broken after all, but it was very bruised and there were partly healed bite marks all over it.

All of his body was covered in sand and drying salt and she could see seaweed, sand and shells tangled into his hair and beard. Although he made no sound in reply she continued to talk gently to him and he relaxed and even smiled a little. Dora saw that before she could help his wounded arm she really needed to get it clean. She went and got the special seat on wheels that Brian had used, and the merman was able to help her get him into it. She wheeled him to the wet room and turned on the shower making sure it was on cool. She gently massaged shampoo into his hair and beard and they both watched the sea debris roll off of him and down the drain. She added conditioner to the matted hair and made sure it was well rinsed. She wheeled him back to the settee wrapped in towels. Almost at once his eyes flickered shut and he went to sleep.

Hoping he would sleep for a while she grabbed her purse and rushed up to the local supermarket. She went straight to the fish counter and perused what was on offer. Forgetting her financial state she bought a beautiful mackerel, raw prawns and four very expensive oysters.

He was still asleep when she got home, so she placed the food on a big dish and sat by him until he woke. He was startled, eyes wide as he saw her and then the plate of fishes. She held it to him and he slowly took an oyster, opening it easily with his healthy hand. He tipped the oyster into his mouth and quickly ate two more. The fourth one he offered to her, opening it first, then holding it to her lips. She was not a big fan of them, but she ate the oyster smiling as she did so. She refused any more and watched fascinated as his sharp teeth stripped the mackerel to the bone and as he chewed each raw prawn, then drinking the water she had poured for him.

Still talking all the time she gently looked at his arm and put some antiseptic on it. She massaged the shoulder and the back of his neck. When she finished she looked at him and saw that he was asleep again.

She sat next to him and he moved in his sleep and put his head on her lap.

They stayed like that for a long time. He sound asleep and her looking out the window to the sea as the light faded and the tide came back in. Since Brian had died Dora had kept herself busy, always on the go, leaving her no time to think and be sad. But here with this head on her lap she had nothing to do but to think. For the first time she thought about Brain, right from when they met, to the last few horrible weeks as his strength was taken. A couple of tears ran down her cheek as she remembered all the good things. Their meeting, marriage, children, holidays, there had been so many good times. He really had been the love of her life and she missed him dreadfully.

The merman finally woke as the moonlight was shining across the sea. He sat up and reached for the wheelchair. It was time to go.

Dora helped him into it and made the difficult trek across the grass and sand to the water's edge. The sea was quite high up the beach and she helped him to the edge. Before she let him go he put his arms around her and embraced her. Then he turned back to the sea and started to roll towards the waves. In seconds he was able to swim and he turned just once and waved at her. She stood on the beach her eyes straining to see him in the moonlight as he went further out to sea.

He was gone.

Tony lived next door to Dora, he had just taken his Labrador for a last walk and went in his own front door.

'Is Dora alright? he asked his wife. 'I've just seen her going in the front door with Brian's wheelchair.'

'I expect she's just got it back from someone she lent it to.' His wife replied.

Tony shook his head. It seemed unlikely to him.

Numbers

(Agonizingly awful alliteration)

One weary washerwoman woefully working weekdays, with wriggling weasel's wet white winter waistcoats.

Two temperamental tailors taping tiny twitching tadpole tails to tattered, terribly torn, Tyrolean trousers.

Three thuggish thieves thoroughly thrilling theatre throngs, then thoughtlessly threatening thirsty thespians.

Four faithful female florists filling forty-five fireproof flats with fancy fresh flowers fortnightly for financing fripperies.

Five fantastically fierce French fishermen frightening floating fishes for friends Friday's family fishy fry-ups.

Six sulky shop-keeping spinster sisters slowly slicing somebody's salmon spread sandwich snacks.

Seven secret spy-catchers skillfully stalking surprisingly short skirted Sunday school secretaries.

Eight ailing aviators aping an ancient Arabic acrobat and achieving aching ankles and ambulance arrival.

Nine naughty night nurses nattering noisily near ninety nifty knicker knitters nearing nausea.

Ten troubled time travelers telling tittle-tattle to trick tired toffee tasters, to take tempting tea time treats.

One-armed Bandit

Brian didn't mean to be a one-armed bandit. In fact he didn't mean to start on his crime spree at all, it just sort of happened.

He'd spent three hours in Casualty, waiting for an x-ray only to be told that his fall has resulted in just a sprained wrist. He was given strapping and a sling, a prescription for pain killers and shown the door.

He went to the pharmacy and had to sign the 'over 60' part of the prescription which proved difficult as it was his right wrist and he was right-handed. It was only as he got into his son's car that he realised that he had accidentally taken the pharmacy's pen. He'd put it into his sling so that he could hand the prescription over. It wasn't worth going back, so he just went home and forgot about it.

Until the next day.

He popped out to the nearby shop and was deciding whether to have a tin of sardines or if he could afford red salmon. An idea got into his head and just wouldn't go away. He slipped the salmon tin into his sling and went and paid for the sardines.

That night he enjoyed the salmon in crusty rolls and his cat enjoyed the sardines. When they were both wiping their whiskers and feeling very content, he promised himself that he wouldn't do it again.

The next day it was a pack of paté, he and the cat enjoyed that too.

His wrist was feeling a lot better the next morning, but he put the sling on anyway, just in case. In the greengrocers he stashed away a pack of asparagus and in the pet shop, some of the cat's favourite treats.

In the days that followed, each day something small and expensive found its way into the sling. It started to get easy, and he started to get greedy.

The supermarket manager's office was smaller than he expected. The manager was surprisingly kind and apparently accepted his story. He had found carrying the wire basket too heavy and put the small pack of the best coffee in the sling and forgotten it.

Numbers

His doddery old man act was so good that in a few minutes they brought him tea and biscuits and an offer to ring his son. The refreshments were welcome, but he was a bit panicky about having his son told. He knew his father wasn't forgetful and although he could lie to the shop staff easily, he wouldn't be able to lie and still look his son in the eye.

He insisted he was all right, paid for the coffee, drank his tea and got away from the supermarket as quickly as he could.

At home he stopped at his wheelie bin and put the sling in it. His short, but exciting life of crime was over. He let himself in, greeted the cat, put the kettle on and retrieved the biscuits he had stuffed in his pocket in the supermarket's office. He was surprised to find the manager's pen in there as well.

But it really wouldn't be worth taking it back.

Poem and Story – The Witch Is Dead.

The Witch Is Dead - Story

Anyone passing by would think that the cottage was completely derelict. The garden was overgrown with vicious brambles and the cottage had cracked filthy windows and a huge hole was evident in the roof.

In fact until a few weeks before it was the home of 'Old Jessie', who was better known in the village as 'The old witch'.

No-one has seen her for ages, but no-one was really bothered. In fact she was dead, and had been for quite a while. Her black cat had squeezed out of the badly fitting front door and was easily making a new life for himself in the local pub, successfully begging scraps from the evening diners.

Jessie's other familiar, a large brown crusty toad, was having the time of his life, feasting on the flies that were hatching out from the maggots that were crawling all over the rubbish bin. Jessie had obviously been working on a spell and the bin was overflowing with eyeless frogs and newts, legless spiders, tongueless larks and stinking herb leaves including rue, belladonna and mandrake.

What remained of Jessie herself was lying where she fell, on the filthy kitchen floor, her spell book still open under her head. A cup lay by her side, the red liquid it had once held, had soaked into the wooden slats. Jessie's gnarled fingers with her long claw like nails were pointing to her own dead eyes, which looked like little black stones shining in her bluish face. If anything she looked happier and healthier in death than she had in life. The lines on her face had softened and she didn't look so old at all. Her tangled hair was still raven black without a trace of grey.

For the first few days she just looked peaceful.

Months later a sign was put up outside the cottage.

'For Sale by Auction.'

It was some time later when the cameras came to record 'Homes Under the Hammer' for the BBC. It was the last in the series.

The Witch was Dead - poem

The Witch was dead
The horror when we went inside
Was to find her body still there
                                putrefied.

Her skin was purple and blue
With hints of green beneath
Her brown skull showed her awful smiling, snarling
                                                        teeth

The stench was so awful
We all felt faint and sick
So we went to open a grimy window
                                quick.

On the windowsill was an enormous toad
His tongue shooting out catching flies.
That crawled on him and everything
                                that dies.

The witch's spell book, dropped on the floor
Open at a page of potions, snails and bugs
But the edges had been eaten away by slimy smelly
                                                        slugs.

The revolting overflowing rubbish bin
With maggots was positively heaving
We turned to go, all we wanted to be was
                                        leaving.

The cottage isn't there any more
There's nothing more to be said
We won't be going back even though we know
The witch is
                                dead.

Questions from the Beach

The waves crashed onto the car roof sounding like a medieval bombardment of huge rocks. For a few moments we were unable to see through the window. As it cleared, dirty water stuck on the windows in spite of the rain and huge streaks ran down out of our view. The water looked brown and oily. Shuddering, we drove slowly away before it could hit us again. The car was filthy and would have to be washed very soon. The small person in the back said 'Nanna, why is the sea so angry?'

I tried to explain about the high tide and the storm, but he really was too young to understand.

Another day we parked the car at the same place in glorious sunshine and went down the sea wall steps to the beach. We stumbled over the pebbles to reach the water's edge. Leaving our shoes on a breakwater we walked along the edge letting the white bubbly foam nibble at our toes. The sea looked shallow as far as we could see and with the sun shining on it, it looked like a huge glass mirror. The small person giggled with delight as the sea tickled his feet and he dug his toes into the sand.

'Nanna.' he said, 'Is this the same sea as when we was nearly drownded?'

I told him it was, but he really was too young to understand.

Just a few days later we were watching the news on television when we saw a stranded ship, off our coast. A helicopter circled overhead and two lifeboats were trying to find members of the crew that had been thrown into the water. A very serious announcer told us that three seamen had died and two had been lifted just in time from the swirling angry sea. The small person watched with interest, because he likes helicopters, but he made no comment.

I do know about the tides, and the storm, and the reasons, but I have to admit that I am also too young to understand.

RT - The Cat who isn't Basil

He's on my lap now,
The cat who isn't Basil
He's not asleep, but on my lap
Proving that he is superior to the others
With a smug grin on his face
And his eyes are almost shut.
Basil would lie across my lap
Totally relaxed, and he'd sleep.

Basil's fur was like an expensive grey silk cravat.
The cat who isn't Basil is rough and orange
With cinnamon stripes, like a cheap toy.
Basil was a super friend
Who shared every emotion.
The cat who isn't Basil is selfish.
He keeps his cat secrets to himself.

Basil always came with soft paws
His claws tucked tidily away,
The cat who isn't Basil uses his claws
Like grappling hooks.
He's purring now
The cat who isn't Basil,
And he'd like me to rub
The only soft bit of fur he has,
Between his shoulder blades.
I do love this cat who isn't Basil.

But he isn't Basil.

She Held Him

She held him just the once
On a starry night
In a golden field
With crowds cheering
Not far away.
And music playing from open windows.
She held him just the once.
With his blue eyes smiling
And his breathing heavy
Tasting of tobacco and peppermint gum.
And she trembled at his touch
And she loved him then with quick abandon
And he loved her with passion and strength.
And the rough feel of his uniform
Rubbed her skin till she laughed.
She held him just the once
Till they sent him away in the morning
And she didn't know his name.

She held him just the once
On a summer's night
In a hospital ward
With nurses talking
Not far away.
And dawn light coming through dusty windows.
She held him just the once.
With his blue eyes on hers
And his breathing, like a whisper
And his skin like silk
Smelling soap and baby powder.
And she trembled as she touched him
And she loved him then with total despair
And he loved her with natural instinct.
And the soft feel of his shawl
Touched her cheek as she cried.
She held him just the once
Till they took him away in the morning
And she never gave him a name.

The Road

The three faded rockers sat gloomily at a messy pub table, four pints of bitter and empty crisp wrappers in front of them. They were still wearing their biker gear, with plenty of leather, chains and studs, but without the crash helmets, as none of them still possessed a motor bike. They were waiting for Steve and he was late as usual. They had all promised their women folk that they wouldn't be late back tonight and now Steve, who didn't have a woman to go home to, was making them late. They were on to a second pint each when he arrived looking as gloomy as they did.

He threw the local paper down in front of them, it was open and across the page the headline read 'Is this the end of the road for The Road?'

'Well.' John said, 'It's a good question isn't it?'

Steve shrugged and downed his stale pint in a few gulps.

'I do have a bit of an idea.' he said. They looked at him. He had been their leader ever since the start and he knew that if he didn't come up with a plan they really had reached the end of the road.

They had played music together since the late sixties and in fact were still mostly playing the same sixties songs that they had started with. Steve had come up with the name 'The Road' one drunken night in 1966 and they still used it. They had never made it big, they'd had a few chances and promises but they'd all came to nothing. So they'd all had other jobs, but somehow kept the group going through girlfriends, wives, children and lately even grandchildren. They'd had a few changes in their line-up, for some reason bass guitarists had come and gone, and Pete had even gone to Australia for four years, but he'd fitted back in again as soon as he came home.

They were a lot older now, retired, or retiring, so they had more spare time, but less hair and absolutely no ambition left. They didn't bother to learn new songs any more and they just played a gig once a week in their local pub 'The Lazy Cow' on Friday nights.

It was in 'The Lazy Cow' that they were sitting now, waiting for Steve to come up with his miracle plan. The pub was old and creaky, as was the landlord, and they were both giving up. The landlord was going to move in with his daughter by the sea, and when he tried to sell the pub, a survey revealed that the building was unsafe and it was beyond repair. It was going to come down and the land turned into 'affordable housing'.

As well as being where the group played their music it was also where they kept their equipment. No-one had room in their homes for their drum kit, guitars, stage gear, amplifiers or the keyboard.

They had another round of drinks and looked at Steve.

'Well.' he said finally 'My mate Barry is giving up his window cleaning round and his van is for sale.'

'Not that old orange pile of rust?'

'Well, yes it won't pass the MOT, but he only wants fifty quid for it and we can just SORN it and park it up.'

'And?'

'And keep all our gear in it. Use it like a shed. If we get a gig we'll just have to take taxis to get there and add it on the price.'

They looked at him, making sure that he was being serious. They had trusted him before, and look where that had got them. Sitting in a condemned pub preparing for what was possibly their last gig. They remembered their womenfolk and their promise to only have one drink and got up to go.

'OK Steve, we'll leave it up to you.'

Steve got up too. He took the empty glasses to the bar and said goodnight to the landlord who was sitting gloomily on a bar stool reading Steve's local paper. 'See you Friday.' he said. 'There should be a good crowd in for our last night.'

Friday night the pub was packed out. The landlord had got in some food and the beer flowed like water. On the small stage 'The Road' was playing their entire repertoire. They had just finished one of his favourites, 'The House of the Rising Sun', when a pretty girl went over to Steve who was taking a drink between songs. She was only a young thing but very pretty.

'Do you do parties?' she asked.

'Well yes, we can do.' he said.

'I'm eighteen next month.' she said 'Me dad was going to pay for a disco, but I'd rather have you – would you come for two hundred and fifty quid?'

Stunned he replied 'We could negotiate the price.' For years they had been playing in The Lazy Cow just for free beer.

'Hey guys.' Steve said to the band, 'I think 'The Road' is back on the road – stick with me and I'll make you famous.'

They all laughed as they played the first few bars of 'Keep on Running.'

Under my bed.

I think there's a monster under my bed.

In fact I know there's a monster under my bed because I put him there. When my daughter was very small she woke up screaming one night and the only way I could pacify her and get her off to sleep was to take the 'Monster' by the hand, give him a stern talking to, lead him out of her bedroom, and put him under my bed, and tell him to stay there and never come out.

He's not really much of a problem although he takes ball point pens, stamps on them and takes out the ink tube. He also hides hair slides, odd socks, remote controls, pairs of scissors, books and important letters. In the far corner he keeps possibly the largest collection of scrunched up tissue hankies known to man.

The cats don't like him much and sometimes I hear them having an argument. Well I can hear the cats scratching the underneath of the bed and making weird growly noises, so I imagine they're not the best of buddies.

The cats and the monster get on much better with the flying dragon that lives in the airing cupboard. He's actually a great asset. His fiery nature keeps it nice and warm and on windy winter nights the steady rhythm of his breathing is very comforting.

I have to leave the door open so that the cats can get in to sleep on him, but he never comes out in an aggressive way. He's been in there since another stormy night when my daughter heard him rattling the windows and wouldn't stay in her bedroom until I ordered him out.

More annoying for me anyway is the troll in the wardrobe. He slides my clothes off their coat hangers and leaves them screwed up in a heap at the bottom of the wardrobe and then he lets the cats in so that they can leave claw marks and fur on my best clothes. No matter how carefully I close the door he clicks it open, just enough to let a cat's paw get round it. He knows when I'm in a hurry too, and hides the item that I'm looking for. He's been in there since I read the story of the 'Three Billy Goats Gruff' to my daughter one night and she couldn't sleep until I took him out.

I was delighted that my daughter had such a good imagination, she'll make a good writer one day, although I'm sorry to say that I drew the line at keeping the grizzly bear she saw in the garden. I'm afraid I just shouted at him till he leapt over the fence and was gone.

Of course, my daughter has left home now and only sleeps in her bedroom on the occasional weekend when she is down from London. I keep quiet about the monster and his friends still being here because now she's a sophisticated twenty year old, I don't think she's afraid of anything.

I sometimes think that I'm being silly and should forget all about them, but they are such a comfort to me, I'd really miss them if they were gone.

And last night I heard a sound in the loft. I'm not sure what it was moving about, but I'm certainly not going up to find out. I spoke to my daughter on the phone and she said that it was probably just a poltergeist. I'm quite happy for him, or her, to stay. In my opinion it's the more the merrier.

Vikings - Another poem and story.

Vikings - Poem

Viking
Invaders
Killing.
Intruding.
Nothing shared.
Grabbing and
Slaughtering.

Violating.
Impulsively
Kidnapping
Indiscriminately.
No Norsemen scared.
Gore and fear.

Victims
Impotent.
Knowing death
Inevitable.
Nobody spared.

Vicious
Invaders
Killing
Insatiably.

Viking
Invaders
Killing.

Viking
Invasion.

Vikings - Story.

He trudged wearily behind the others, getting further back with every step. He'd broken a leg when he was a child and it had left him with a slight limp, which made his progress on the slippery muddy ground, painfully slow as they moved away from the coast. As the night went on he could no longer see the others in the moonlight or hear their voices and the earth gradually became rock hard under his feet as a heavy frost settled.

He felt totally alone and lost. He kept walking to stay warm, but had no idea where he was going.

Suddenly he heard a sound that made every hair on his head stand on end. Goose pimples covered his arms and he stopped walking. He knew at once what the sound was. It was the sound of a new born baby's first cry.

He followed the sound to a small hut beside a huge tree. He could see smoke rising from the roof emerging into the clear crisp night.

He peered through the doorway and as his eyes became accustomed he saw a sight that filled his eyes with tears. Inside were two women, sisters he thought, and one was handing a tightly wrapped crying infant to the other.

Viking or not he let out an uncontrollable sob and the women looked at him.

The last time he had heard that sound was when his wife had given birth to their tiny daughter. He'd then had to watch helplessly as his wife had bled to death. He shuddered as he remembered how afterwards he had wrapped his baby up and run around the village trying to find a woman to take her on and feed her. No-one had helped and the baby had died the next day.

He stood now in the doorway quite unable to move.

The woman who was standing beckoned him in and said something he didn't understand. He went inside crouching down because of the low entrance.

There was a fire burning in the middle of the hut and the warmth surprised him. He hadn't realised how cold he was.

The woman holding the baby was lying down on a makeshift bed raised off the mud floor. She smiled at him and spoke too. He sat down and gently touched the baby's head with his hand.

The baby had fallen silently asleep, but in the firelight he couldn't take his eyes from its sleeping face. The standing woman dipped some wooden bowls in a pot that was over the fire and placed one in his hands. It was hot and warming and tasted delicious. He had been on a fish diet since they had left home and this broth was made from some kind of bird, there were small sharp bones that he, like the women, sucked the meat off and threw them into the fire where they crackled.

He didn't remember falling asleep, but hours later he woke to the sound of the baby contentedly suckling. Sunlight was streaming into the hut and he could for the first time look around. He could then see that the women were not sisters, but mother and daughter and they were regarding him with some amusement. He suspected that he had been snoring, but they were still smiling at him.

Someone had put a sacking cover over him and he climbed out of the wooden hut shaking it and himself. There was very little there, the straw roofed hut was leaning against the tree in a small clearing in a thick wood. He felt a strong sense of belonging that he hadn't felt since he'd lost his wife.

There was another hut nearby and two small children were on the edge of the wood collecting sticks.

He knew that these were the people he had come to steal from, but he could see they had so little that there was nothing to steal, and to take their lives was no longer an option.

He didn't decide to stay with them, he just never left. He learned their language and found out that both the women were widows and the baby was a strong healthy boy. He became their provider, friend and protector and never did return to his homeland as he had indeed found his home in this new alien land.

Waiting

Every dusk, whatever the weather, whatever the season, the dog went down the front path and sat at the open gate. He sat, his eyes fixed on the lane looking at the distant fence post where the lane turned into the main road and out of his sight. He sat there unmoving, his eyes alert, his ears cocked for any sound, totally ignoring the birds returning to their roosts, the rabbits emerging from the cover of the verges and the bats swooping low over his head as they caught their insect supper. He stayed unmoving every night until it was too dark to see the post any more. Only then would he go back indoors and settle for the evening.

One summer evening a large van drove down the lane, the house was the only one there and visitors were rare and unexpected. The driver was lost but the dog didn't know that. Excitedly he bounded towards the van but in the twilight the driver didn't see the large black shape hurtling towards his vehicle. He did feel the bump though and stepped out horrified to pick up the lifeless dog and carry it up the path to the front door.

The woman cried many tears that night and in the morning she had to ask someone to help her dig a deep hole under the apple tree. As the shadows lengthened she carried her pet's body and placed it gently in the hole and covered his body, first with her tears and then with earth. Finally she placed a stone on top and painted the dog's name on it.

She went indoors to wash her hands and then she carried the kitchen chair outside.

From that night, whatever the weather, whatever the season, she went down the front path and sat at the open gate. She sat, her eyes fixed on the lane looking at the distant fence post where the lane turned into the main road and out of sight. She sat there unmoving, her eyes alert, listening for any sound, oblivious to the birds returning to their roosts, the rabbits emerging from the cover of the verges and the bats swooping low over her head as they caught their insect supper. She stayed unmoving every night until it was too dark to see the post any more. Only then would she go back indoors and settle for the evening.

X

The X shaped scar on Poppy's right cheek was already beginning to fade when she was well enough to return to school.

Until the accident Poppy and Rosie were identical twins and happily in their first year at school, but the freak accident that had sent a medal rod flying off of a lorry through the window into her face had changed that. The surgeons had done a wonderful job of rebuilding and replacing Poppy's broken facial bones, but it had been a long job a long way from home.

The unbroken bond that they had enjoyed since before birth was smashed and Rosie had felt very neglected while her parents cried and worried and spent hours at the hospital with Poppy. She missed her too, but was more upset by the way she was passed between friends and relatives, often not knowing at school who was going to pick her up, or even where she would be sleeping that night. She had been taken reluctantly to the hospital to visit her sister and been envious of the bedside TV, toys and treats that Poppy was allowed. Poppy had tried to hug her, but Rosie had been horrified by the medical paraphernalia, especially the drips and wires and had pulled away. She had been made to create 'Get Well Soon' cards for her sister when she would rather have been playing and had to talk to her on the phone when she didn't know what to say. There had been many promises of Poppy coming home, but there was always a delay while they did another operation or fought another infection. But, finally the day came and they were once again strapped in, side by side, on the back seat of the new family car on their way home. Poppy had no recollection of the accident and was unafraid, but Rosie tensed every time the traffic slowed ahead in case something should fall from a vehicle. They had previously held hands in the back on the car, but now Rosie ignored the offered hand and clutched a cuddly dog instead.

After a few more days, Poppy was back at school. She had done some lessons in hospital and was not too far behind her classmates, but she was not happy that Rosie had made a lot of new friends and no longer wanted to be her constant companion. Rosie was just fed up with all the fuss that Poppy was receiving. She was not to do PE or dance and at playtime Rosie was to be expected to stay inside with her sister when she would rather be out playing with her friends. Mrs Atkins, their well-intentioned teacher had warned the other children not to stare at Poppy and they responded by not talking to or playing with her at all. This same teacher gave Poppy a place to sit opposite her sister as she thought she would be happy there. She was, but Rosie was not, and refused to sit there and had to be moved. At lunch time Rosie held back and waited until Poppy had joined the dinner line so that she did not have to be near her. In the afternoon the class were first talking about families and home, then followed a story and then they had to return to their places to draw a picture of their homes. The children were soon busy, each one drawing a picture of a traditional child's idea of a house, almost square with four windows and a door in the middle. Mrs Atkins thought it unlikely that they all lived in houses that looked like this, but once they started adding colour and house numbers they started to add more accurate features. She smiled when she saw Poppy and Rosie's pictures, they were identical, with matching blue front doors, a tall scribbly tree on the left and even a shaggy brown dog outside. Mrs Atkins told the children to add their families playing in the garden and soon matchsticky people were being drawn.

Poppy drew herself, her sister and her Mum and Dad. Rosie drew just herself and her parents. It was the only different feature of the two drawings. Mrs Atkins smiled at Rosie 'Don't forget to put Poppy in.' There was laughter in her voice, but her smile faded when she received by way of an answer a stare from Rosie's blue eyes, which then flashed in anger. Snatching up her newly sharpened pencil she stabbed at the picture and tearing the paper, added a huge X across the left side of the house. She then threw the pencil on the floor and stormed across the classroom to the book corner where she dived face down and sobbing into a bean bag cushion. Mrs Atkins sent a child to get help and a teaching assistant arrived and persuaded Rosie to go to the school library for a chat.

Once out of class Rosie's tears vanished and she was happy to talk. She tried to explain her anger at Poppy, and grumpily said that Poppy had made them ugly and they both looked like monsters. 'But Rosie' the teaching assistant explained 'You haven't changed at all, you're just as pretty, you have gorgeous blond hair and very blue eyes and Poppy is starting to look just as pretty as you again.'

Rosie looked at the teaching assistant as if she was crazy. She knew what Poppy looked like, she'd been looking at Poppy face since they were born and she knew that their faces should look the same. All she saw now was that ugly pink scar across her face and the tiny bumps on the skin in front of her ears, and the hair. Poppy's had been cut shorter in hospital and no longer reached to her waist although their mother had tied both of their hair back into ponytails with identical ribbons.

The school sent for their mother. She was horrified about what had been said and on the drive there was cross with Rosie. But when she saw her tear stained face waiting outside the school office she held her close in an embrace. They were called into the headteacher's office as she kindly suggested that Rosie needed to talk about her feelings and perhaps the school could arrange something. It was decided that this would happen and Rosie's mother took her home.

Later that afternoon, Rosie was sent into a neighbour's house while Poppy was also picked up from school. She knew the neighbour well, she had been left there many times while Poppy had been in hospital. There were older children living there who were still at school and Rosie asked if he could go into Freddie's bedroom to look at his cars and model planes.

'As long as you don't touch anything.' the neighbour said.

The twin's mother knocked on the door when she got back with Poppy and was chatting to the neighbour who had sent Poppy up to her son's bedroom to tell Rosie that it was time to go home. It was Poppy's screams that silenced them. They echoed round the house seeming to bounce off the walls. The adults feet seemed to be stuck to the floor as they tried to climb the stairs. Poppy was still just inside the door screaming and they had to push her out the way so that they could see Rosie. Very calmly she looked at them, her face just a mass of blood. She had found the Stanley Knife that Freddie used in his model making. She had drawn it across her left cheek to form a large open gash forming an X.

The hospital staff had been brilliant, the cuts were not too deep and the doctor who put in very tiny neat stitches promised that there would be no permanent scars. They kept Rosie in overnight but she was allowed home the next day. Just hours later their mother found them happily chatting away, playing with their Peppa Pig toys. They again looked the mirror image of each other and when their mother heard them laughing she felt that maybe it was the beginning of their lives getting back to normal.

Yuletide Story

In spite of his warm red coat and hood he could feel the damp and chill as soon as he entered the house. If possible, it felt colder indoors than the December outside air. It was darker too. Outside the moon was full and bright stars filled the sky. Inside there were no lights, not even the glow from modern technology on stand-by that enabled him to see in most modern houses.

Inside the house smelt awful. There was an overwhelming stench of mould mixed with the familiar smell of the results of stale human bodily functions. There was silence too, a loud silence that made his ears ring with the effort of trying to hear something.

He pointed his torch around the room and found the light switch. He turned the light on and a bare low power light bulb showed him the room. Shabby didn't really cover the state of the house. Papers strewn around, clothes, washed and unwashed, covered most surfaces and dirty crockery and food were all over a small table in the middle of the room. An overflowing ash tray was balanced precariously on the edge of a stained and ragged settee.

Trying to ignore the state of the room, and the smell, he consulted his list. There should be two little girls living here, but the cold silent room had no toys or signs of them, apart from the little bags, obviously containing used nappies. And the smell!

There was a battered door leading to another room and he went and opened it, quite fearful of what he would find. With that light on too he could see that there was a bed and an empty cot and a pile of dirty clothes on the floor. A movement attracted his attention and he could suddenly see a tiny tear stained face amongst the stained bedding. A child made a whimpering sound and he uncovered it to reveal that it was a girl wearing just a grey vest and pink knickers. Her hair was matted and her arms and legs stick thin. Tear stains marked her face and her huge eyes stared up at him. In her arms was what he thought was a doll, but when he touched the child's cold skin, he realised that she was cuddling a baby. He picked them both up, sat down on the edge of the bed and gently put them on his lap. The child made the little whimpering sound again. The baby moved and he was so relieved that tears filled his eyes. He had thought that it was dead.

The girl started to cry and he held her close so that she could share the warmth in his coat. He wrapped the baby in too and held them both close.

He took out his mobile phone and dialled 999 asking for the police and an ambulance. He sat, rocking the children, and waited until the blue lights flashing appeared outside, their lights filled the rooms around some torn old lace curtains.

He gently patted each child to reassure them and then he opened the front door so that the police and medics could get in. He placed two wrapped presents, a soft teddy for the baby and a cuddly dog for the child, into the children's arms.

As the police and paramedics entered he disappeared up the chimney to carry on with his deliveries, a little late, but feeling good. He picked up the reins and stirred the dozing reindeer into life.

Zebras and Tigers

This last item is neither a story nor a poem but an insight into children's minds. I have been privileged to work with children and could probably write a small book about their wisdom.

I could tell the story of the girl with a loud voice who asked me what colour to make the butterfly's testicles. They were tentacles, honest. Or the hysterical boy whose coat was missing from his peg at home time. He was wearing it.

But I really have to go for the best answer to a question that I have ever received. We were writing poems about animals and a seven year old boy was writing that a tiger was chasing a zebra to kill and eat it. With all my adult knowledge of where animals live I told him that this could not happen and asked him if he could think why. He thought for a very long time, his eyes looking in all directions for help. Finally, he put his answer together. 'I think' he said 'that things with stripes never eat other things with stripes, because the stripes put them off.'

I think he maybe was right.

And finally there was another boy. Instead of the work we were supposed to be doing we were talking about cats. He told me the age, colour and name of his new kitten. 'Is it a boy or a girl?' I asked. 'We don't know.' he said, 'We're waiting to see if it lays any eggs.'

Ruth Partis

Ruth Partis has been writing stories and poems most of her life, but her work was only suitable for publication with the invention of the word- processor and the spell-check. Now retired from her work in education and journalism she is discovering the joys of being a grandmother. Ruth has a very supportive husband and three grown-up children of whom she is justifiably proud. She has lived on the Isle of Sheppey for more than forty years, but can still get lost due to her appalling sense of direction.